The Gymkhana

WOODLEY FARM

The road was blocked here

Road to the Fire Station

The Town

Where the fire was

RIVER

The green parcel was dropped here

Hyde Heath
THE FINISH OF THE RALLY

GUMDROP
at the Rally

written and illustrated by
VAL BIRO

FOLLETT PUBLISHING COMPANY
CHICAGO   F   NEW YORK

Copyright © 1968 by Val Biro. First published 1968 by Brockhampton Press, Ltd., Leicester.

Published 1969 in the United States of America by Follett Publishing Company, Chicago.
All rights reserved. No portion of this book may be reproduced in any form
without written permission from the publisher.

SBN 695-43620-1 Titan binding
SBN 695-83620-X Trade binding

Library of Congress Catalog Card Number: 69-10802

First Printing E

THERE WAS A STRANGE SIGHT at the Red Lion one
sunny morning in June. The vintage cars had come to
start their big rally of the year. Never was there such a
collection of fine old cars in the yard. Each had a
rally number fixed to it.

Number 1 was an Alvis Duck-Back, and Number 2 a
Morris Bullnose. The Model-T Ford was Number 3,
the Speed-Six Bentley 4. Number 5 was a two-seater
Dodge, and Number 6 was an Alfa-Romeo. The small
Humber was Number 7, and the big Renault was 8.

And then there was a blue car, with a black hood and a brass horn. It was Number 9: an Austin Clifton Heavy Twelve-Four, vintage 1926, driven by Bill McArran. It was Gumdrop.

Bill's wife, Sally, was there too, to be Gumdrop's navigator and to show Bill the way at the rally.

GHRAUPP! went the organizer's claxon. Everyone was silent. "You will follow the instructions," he said, "and watch out for signposts. Make sure that you stay on the right road. If you don't, you'll lose points. Cars will start at one-minute intervals, drive for sixty miles and finish at Hyde Heath. The first car to arrive at four o'clock will be the winner. And don't get lost!"

HONK-HONK! went Gumdrop's horn, when at last it was his turn to start. Bill drove for ten miles, carefully following the right road according to the instructions that Sally read out. Then they came to a cross-roads. "Which way now?" asked Bill.

"Thataway!" shouted a young man by the roadside.

"Thanks!" said Bill, and drove down a bumpy road. It twisted and it turned. It was steep and it was narrow. It turned again and then, by a gate, it stopped.

"This *can't* be the way," Sally said.

"That chap back there must have fooled us," said Bill. "We must turn round now, and look for the right road."

TOOTLE-TOOT! went a little
horn. Bill stopped Gumdrop.
There, in the road, was a small
boy in a pedal car. He was crying.
"I'm tired," he said. "And I think
I'm lost. My name is Peter and I
live at Mapletree Farm."

"That's the farm down the road," said
Sally. "I noticed the name as we went past."
"Right," said Bill to the small boy, "we'll put your car
in Gumdrop and take you home."

MOOO! went the cows at Mapletree Farm when they
saw Peter again, and the donkey said EEYAAW. The
farmer was also glad to see Peter back, and to show how
pleased he was he gave Bill a can of oil for Gumdrop
and asked if they would have a cup of coffee.

"Thank you very much," said Bill, "but we can't stay.
We must turn round now and look for the right road."

They turned left,
and they turned right,
and they drove for miles, searching.
Then they heard a loud NEEEEIGH!
It was a pony in a trailer.
"Our car broke down," said the little
girl in jodhpurs, "and we must get to
the gymkhana in time for the
jumping competition. Could
you please take us?"

"Jump in!" said Bill. "We'll hitch the trailer to Gumdrop and get you to the show in time."

And they did get there in time,
just as the starting bell went CLANG!
Soon it was the little girl's turn to ride
around. Her pony jumped so well
that they won a rosette.

"You have been very kind,"
said the girl's father to
Bill and Sally, and to show
how pleased he was he gave
them a set of sparking-plugs for
Gumdrop and asked them if they would
like to stay and see some more jumping.

"Thank you very much," said Bill, "but we must turn
round now and look for the right road."

This time they turned right,
and then left, and drove on
for miles, searching.
They found themselves in a town,
where all the bells were going
DING-DONG-DOINNG!

The streets were crowded and there were strange
vehicles driving slowly along. It was a carnival
procession. There was no room to turn, so Gumdrop
had to drive slowly along with them.

Just then a man ran up to Gumdrop. "Please do us the favor, sir, of conveying His Worship the Mayor to the Town Hall in your exquisite vehicle. His official car has unfortunately developed a puncture."

"My word, it is a pleasure to ride in an original Twelve-Four again," said the Mayor. "I had just such a car myself when I was young," he said. And they drove among the cheering crowds.

"My grateful thanks to you both," said the Mayor when they reached the Town Hall. And to show how pleased he was, he gave Bill his old authentic Heavy Twelve-Four instruction book and driving manual for Gumdrop, and asked them if they would stay for lunch.

"Thank you very much," said Bill, "but we must turn round now and look for the right road."

They turned left,
and then right,
and out of the town.
They drove on for
miles, searching.
Then they stopped.

The road was blocked by a tractor. "Please help!" cried
the driver, Mr. Woodley. "I was on my way to market,
but the door of my trailer burst open and all the piglets
got away! They must have scampered back to my farm."

Mr. Woodley got into the back seat of Gumdrop, and they drove after the piglets.

Mr. Woodley found four piglets in a pond.

Sally found three in the shed.

Bill found two in the bathtub.

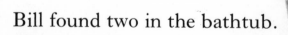

And the last one was in a barrel.

They put them all into Gumdrop and took them back to the trailer. The piglets went SQUEEEEEK-SQUEEEEK!

"Thank you for rounding
them up," said Mr. Woodley.
And to show how pleased he was,
he gave Bill a set of vintage tools
for Gumdrop, which were in his tractor.

"Thank you very much," said Bill. "We must turn
round now and look for the right road."

It was getting late now. They turned right, then left, then right again, still searching for the right road. Then, at a cross-roads they saw a signpost. It was pointing to Hyde Heath, where the rally was to finish. "We've found the right road at last," said Sally to Bill.

Just then, they heard a CRACKLE, SIZZLE, CRACKLE and saw a cloud of black smoke. "That hayrick's on fire!" cried Bill, "and there's nobody at the farm!"

Hyde Heath 5

There was only one thing to do.
Bill turned Gumdrop around again and
drove back to the town to call the fire-brigade.

CLANG-CLANG, CLANG-CLANG! went the fire-engine, and HONK-HONK! went Gumdrop, as he led the firemen back to the blaze. The hayrick was burning furiously, but the buildings were still unharmed. The firemen unrolled the hoses and put the fire out in no time.

Just then the owner of the farm returned, and to show
how pleased he was, he gave Bill a genuine vintage
two-gallon gas tin for Gumdrop.
"Thank you very much," said Bill.
Then he turned to Sally. "We
really must go on now
and finish the rally."

They drove on for two miles, when they heard a GR-GRRRRHHR, getting louder.

A motor-bike came furiously towards them. It had to brake hard when it saw Gumdrop— SCREEEEECH!—it swerved left, it lurched right, it skidded left again, and it dropped a parcel from the back.

But it didn't crash, and it didn't stop. With an alarmed glance at Gumdrop, the rider kicked down a gear, accelerated fast and roared away.

"It's that chap with the long hair again!" cried Bill. "The one who fooled us this morning. And look! He dropped his parcel!" By this time the motor-bike was far out of sight. So Bill picked up the parcel and put it on the back seat. Then they drove on to the rally.

The other cars were already there when they arrived.
Gumdrop was last, because Bill and Sally had not
found the right road.

GHRAUPP-GHRAUPP! went the organizer's claxon.
"Ladies and gentlemen," he announced, "the
rally is now over, but we can't
give out the prizes because
they've been stolen!"

"Stolen!" cried Bill.
Then he remembered
the parcel. He got it out and
opened it. And there, sure enough,
were the three shiny silver cups!

"Wonderful!" cried the organizer. "The thief has been foiled, and we can award the prizes after all. And though Gumdrop hasn't won a silver cup, I give him this brass starting-handle as a special prize for solving the crime!"

Everyone cheered, and all the cars sounded their horns: GLUUURK-GUG and BLEEP-BLIP; HONK-TONK and TOOTLE-TOOT!

So that was the end of the rally. Gumdrop was the last car, but everybody cheered him. He didn't find the right road, but he helped a lost little boy,

a girl with a pony, a mayor in a procession,

and a farmer with ten little pigs.

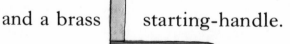

He also helped to put out a fire, and he found the silver cups. He didn't win a cup himself, but just the same he was given

a can of oil, a set of sparking-plugs,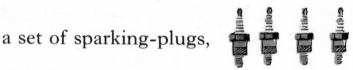

an authentic Twelve-Four instruction book and driving

manual, a set of vintage tools,

 a genuine vintage two-gallon gas tin

and a brass starting-handle.

Gumdrop was the happiest vintage car at the rally.